Richard Wagner, 1813–1883

From the Ring of the Nibelung, book one. Illustration by Gil Kane.

RICHARD WAGNER'S

THE
RING
OF THE NIBELUNG

ADAPTED BY ROY THOMAS
ART BY GIL KANE
COLORED BY JIM WOODRING
LETTERED BY JOHN COSTANZA

THE RING OF THE NIBELUNG

Copyright © 1989, 1991 DC Comics Inc. All Rights Reserved

All characters, their distinctive likenesses and related indicia featured in this publication are trademarks of DC Comics Inc. The stories, characters and incidents featured in this publication are entirely fictional.

Published by arrangement with DC Comics Inc.,
1325 Avenue of the Americas, New York, NY 10019
Warner Books, Inc., 666 Fifth Avenue, New York, NY 10103

A Time Warner Company
Printed in Canada
First Warner printing, September 1991

FOREWORD

Adapting Richard Wagner's four-opera *Der Ring des Nibelungen* into comic-book format was a double-edged undertaking, both natural and foolhardy.

Retelling great adventures, true or fictional, has long been a staple of sequential art. Ever since man has been having adventures he has recorded them in some kind of illustrated form, from cave walls to hieroglyphics to daily newspaper strips . . . in comic books.

Operas had been rendered in comics before, but The Ring Cycle was a tall order—maybe the tallest. Brimming with images of heroes and gods, of dragons and magic, of love and battles, Wagner's tetralogy seemed the very essence upon which so much of comic books is based; however, the combined operas were close to sixteen hours long. If ever a tale could be termed "epic," it was this.

What's more, we obviously could not show the music. By adapting the operas themselves we would draw attention to that fact. Lost would be each overture, each "aria". Attempting to translate the inspiring majesty of "The Ride of the Valkyries" alone would seem reason enough to abandon the endeavor from the start. We wanted to do them justice and not merely be an annotated retelling.

It might have been easier to derive the stories from the original legends: the *Nibelungenlied*, the *Volsungasaga*, or from the *Elder Edda*, a selection of poems dated around 1300. Even this would have been, to mix mythical metaphors, a herculean task. For these Teutonic epos are not as lyrical as their Roman and Greek counterparts. They are disjunct, cumbersome, somewhat crude. Wagner, one might say, was the Homer that blended these Germanic odes into one concordant song.

So why did we do it? We had two strong points in our favor: Roy Thomas and Gil Kane.

These gentlemen, comic-book professionals with nearly seventy-five years of experience between them, had long had it in their hearts to adapt The Ring. They had

by The Editors

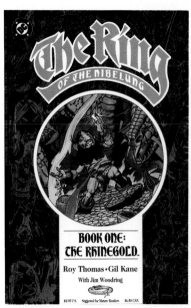

From the Ring of the Nibelung, book one. Illustration by Gil Kane.

Roy Thomas

Gil Kane

both approached DC Comics. Roy and Gil had equal fondness for the material, as well as knowledge of the Icelandic myths—two different perspectives, both valid, both captivating. It is a tribute to these men that their cooperative melding of ideas has brought about this unique vision of the Volsung tale you hold in your hands. Just as the orchestra, set designers, director, and singers bring together the operatic tetralogy by Wagner on the stage, so did Roy, Gil, Jim Woodring, and John Costanza bring together this artistic accomplishment sure to be enjoyed by comic-book reader and opera-lover alike.

So, onward to the great double-edged adventure. We feel we have successfully overcome all the obstacles in the actual storytelling of Richard Wagner's Ring of the Nibelung. And if you feel moved to listen to the operas while partaking of this book, then we've even overcome the lack of music herein. However you read it, if your enjoyment is complete, our undertaking was a success.

About the creative team:

ROY THOMAS has written in every form of the comics medium ever since the mid sixties: super-heroes, western, horror and, most particularly, fantasy or sword-and-sorcery. With humble beginnings in comics fandom, creating and editing his own fanzines (comics fan magazines), he is best known for his adaptation of the works of Robert E. Howard, who created such characters as Conan the Barbarian and Red Sonja. With his fascination for period pieces, Thomas has also made his mark in revitalizing some of the heroes of the 1940s, including DC Comics' hero team The Justice Society. Thomas served well as both editor and editor-in-chief at Marvel Comics in the early 1970s, but never lost sight of his writing. Roy lives in California with his wife.

GIL KANE stands as a leader in graphic storytelling, a hallmark by which so many others can be measured. Beginning in the early 1940s, Kane worked for numerous companies through the years, until the so-called Silver Age of costumed super-heroes when he helped establish Green Lantern and The Atom for DC Comics, then National Periodical Publications. Kane continued at DC as well as Marvel Comics, including working on Conan with Roy

Thomas, Spider-Man, and many others. He has published his own comics, drawn newspaper strips, and has ever been a forerunner in his field. He has won several awards, not the least of which is the Reuben Goldberg Award for Outstanding Achievement in a Story Comic Book. Gil lives in California with his wife.

JIM WOODRING is a skilled painter and quite familiar with the comics medium. More than once he has gone the route of self-publishing, but his work has appeared in BUZZ, among other magazines. He wrote and drew his own magazine, entitled JIM, for Fantagraphics Books. He has also done a great deal of animation work. Jim lives in Seattle with his wife.

JOHN COSTANZA's list of accomplishments could easily fill the next ten pages, as he has lettered just about every DC comic around. His titles, word balloons, and sound effects add to the overall clarity and success of this book ❧

Jim Woodring

INTRODUCTION

by Brian Kellow
Managing Editor
of *Opera News*

Alberich steals Rhine Gold in 1869 engraving of Das Rhinegold *from a Theodor Pixis drawing* . . .

DC Comics' adaptation of Richard Wagner's monumental opera cycle, *Der Ring des Nibelungen*, may raise a few eyebrows—but should it? The Norse and Teutonic legends that Wagner took as his source material are chock full of dragons, gnomes, gods and goddesses: certified comic-book material. But Wagner's *music* is equally ripe material for DC's Gil Kane and Roy Thomas. Is any other composer's work as cinematic as Wagner's? From the sustained E-flat that signals the beginning of the world in *Das Rheingold* to the shattering final moments of *Götterdämmerung*, the *Ring* veritably swims with imagery; one not only hears the music, one *sees* it as well.

It is doubtful that any composer ever faced a more daunting task than Wagner, when, at age thirty-five, he set out to create *Der Ring des Nibelungen*. Adapting the legends into a workable libretto was challenge enough, but Wagner also sought to redefine an entire art form. His previous operas, *Rienzi*, *Der Fliegende Holländer* (The Flying Dutchman), *Tannhäuser* and *Lohengrin* had brought him considerable fame, but each owed something, in varying degreees, to the Italian opera tradition. Wagner longed to create an entirely new musical form beyond the boundaries of conventional opera. His new form, "music drama," would dispense with arias, duets and other set pieces that interrupted the flow of action. Instead, Wagner envisioned a continuous stream of fully integrated musical dialogue. He longed to create the kind of opera where every action, every word, every note would enhance the characterizations and advance the drama. Wagner possessed a fierce nationalistic streak, and wished to enhance his country's cultural profile, which had faded considerably by the mid-nineteenth century. His would be a purely *German* art form. He even envisioned a Wagner festival theater, set up to perform his works exclusively, presenting the finest German singers specially trained in the techniques of music drama.

Wagner found his source material in the ancient Teutonic and Norse sagas. Much of the *Ring* was forged from the *Nibelungenlied,* an early-thirteenth-century epic, and its Norse precursor, *The Edda,* dating from twelfth-century Iceland. *The Edda* contributed to the spirit of the *Ring* as well as to its structure, for it possesses one of the dominant traits of Norse mythology: the implacable presence of death. In this world, doom and destruction await man and god alike. According to the eminent scholar Edith Hamilton:

> The only sustaining support possible for the human spirit, the one pure unsullied good men can hope to attain, is heroism; and heroism depends on lost causes. The hero can prove what he is only by dying. The power of good is shown not by triumphantly conquering evil, but by continuing to resist evil while facing certain defeat. . . . The hero in one of the Norse stories who laughs aloud while his foes cut his heart out of his living flesh shows himself superior to his conquerors. He says to them, in effect, You can do nothing to me because I do not care what you do. They kill him, but he dies undefeated.

One of the most difficult tasks Wagner faced was whittling down the enormous number of characters and plot details. With remarkable economy and skill, he manipulated the myths to accommodate the demands of his music drama. For the most part, he remained true to the legends: the rainbow bridge appears in both legend and opera, and the Siegmund-Sieglinde episode from *Die Walküre* matches up well with the *Volsunga Saga.* Wotan, the god with mortal failings, is also an accurate reflection of the figure in legend. For Brünnhilde and her sister Valkyries, Wagner reached back beyond his literary sources. The Valkyries of Germanic history were warriors and conquerors, the full equals of men. Courage was the most highly prized quality in men and women alike. This was later softened in Nordic poetry of the twelfth and thirteenth centuries, when the Valkyries appeared as visions of death to the male warrior as he expired on the battlefield. These are the Valkyries of the *Nibelungenlied,* but Wagner chose to restore them to the warrior stature that was theirs by right of history.

. . . The Rhinemaidens from same 1869 engraving . . .

. . . which also depicted Fafner and Fasolt carrying Freia.

Sieglinde in Die Walküre *in this newspaper drawing by Knut Ekwall of 1876 Bayreuth production.*

At the same time, Wagner was unafraid of taking liberties with the legends. In the original sources, the Nibelung's gold was not under the Rhine River but buried inside a cave; Siegmund and Sieglinde don't succumb to their forbidden passion but are brought together by Wotan's will. The loudest criticism of Wagner's handling of the myths stemmed from his tendency to strip characters of their nobility—notably Fricka, whom he characterizes less as a goddess defending the rules of the game than as a shrewish, vindictive hausfrau.

In the end, it would take Wagner twenty-six years, from 1848 until 1874, to complete the *Ring*. The librettos were written in reverse order. Originally he intended to write only a single opera, *Siegfrieds Tod* (The Death of Siegfried), which focused only on the hero's final days. When he set about composing the music in 1850, he realized that Siegfried's story needed to be placed in a broader context. The following year, he wrote the text for *Der Junge Siegfried* (Young Siegfried), which convinced him he would need to include the entire narrative. He eventually wrote the libretto of *Die Walküre* and finally of *Das Rheingold*. The music he composed in chronological order.

There were numerous interruptions. In May 1849 he participated in the ill-fated Dresden uprising, which was quelled within one week. Shortly before the Revolution began, an article of Wagner's appeared in a radical Dresden newspaper, calling for the abolition of the old, corrupt political order in Germany. "I will," he wrote, "destroy this order that divides mankind into hostile nations, into powerful and weak, into privileged and outlawed, into rich and poor; for it makes unhappy men of all. I will destroy this order of things that makes millions the slaves of a few, and makes these few the slaves of their own power, their own riches . . . and from the ruins of this old world may a new world arise, filled with undreamed happiness."

Perhaps Wagner was more fearful for his own future than for the future of Germany. The existing political order failed to provide a nurturing atmosphere for his artistic ambitions. Although Wagner never actively joined the fighting, his revolutionary fervor was widely enough known that a warrant was issued for his arrest, and he was forced to flee to Switzerland. He settled in Zurich, joined by his then wife, Minna Planer. He set to work writing essays on his theories, including his seminal work, *Opera and Drama* (1851), and composed the whole of *Das Rheingold* and *Die Walküre*, as well as the first two acts of *Siegfried*.

He set aside work on *Siegfried* in 1857, primarily to concentrate on *Tristan und Isolde*, his passionate tribute to his new love, Mathilde Wesendonk, the wife of one of his benefactors. In 1864 he embarked on his long and convoluted relationship with Ludwig II, the eighteen-year-old King of Bavaria. Ludwig had nursed an obsession with Wagner's music ever since seeing *Lohengrin* three years earlier. When Wagner published his *Ring* texts in 1863, Ludwig proclaimed himself the composer's savior. He paid Wagner's debts and granted him free lodging, a yearly salary and the freedom to create.

Not, however, unconditional freedom. Wagner's arrangement with Ludwig meant that the king owned the *Ring* outright, and it was his wish that the cycle be performed in Munich. While the two men debated the issue, *Tristan und Isolde* had its premiere in Munich in 1865. Already Wagner had run afoul of Ludwig's cabinet, which was suspicious of his quest for a Wagner theater in Munich and, even more critically, of the potential scandal posed by his relationship with Cosima von Bülow.

Cosima was the wife of one of Wagner's disciples, the conductor Hans von Bülow, and the daughter of Wagner's longtime friend and champion, Franz Liszt. Their acquaintance, which began in 1853 when Wagner was forty and Cosima fifteen, blossomed into love in 1863, a mere six years after her marriage to Bülow. In 1864 the Bülows settled in Munich, where Wagner had arranged a court appointment for Bülow. But Ludwig soon became distressed by the nature of Cosima's relationship with Wagner (she already had born him two daughters, Isolde and Eva, while living under the same roof with Bülow). Ludwig's cabinet in turn resented the king's attention being focused on such personal affairs, particularly at a time when Bavaria was on the brink of entering the Austro-Prussian War. Wagner was again branded a troublemaker, and Ludwig requested that he leave Munich for several months. He returned to Switzerland, settling at Villa Triebschen near Lucerne, where in 1867 he completed *Die Meistersinger von*

Wotan and Fricka, again from 1869 Das Rhinegold *engraving of Theodor Pixis drawing . . .*

. . . Mime and Alberich from same engraving.

Nürnberg. The following year Cosima, along with Isolde and Eva, joined him at Triebschen. A son, Siegfried, was born in 1869. In 1870, her divorce from Bülow at last final, Cosima and Wagner were married.

After six years, Wagner and Ludwig continued to debate the location of the *Rheingold* premiere. In the end, Ludwig won the battle but lost the war: *Rheingold* and *Die Walküre* were both staged in Munich in 1869–70, much to Wagner's dissatisfaction. For some time he had been skeptical about the future of German art and culture under Prussian rule, and he became increasingly convinced that the only way to present his works properly was to build a theater specifically designed for the task. Wagner sought, and initially failed to secure, Ludwig's patronage for the project. Many cities bid for the honor of housing Wagner's festival theater, but in the end the composer settled on a rather unremarkable Bavarian town called Bayreuth. The new theater's cornerstone was laid on May 22, 1872. Despite devastating lack of national support for the project, Wagner's fund-raising efforts were aided by the proliferation of Wagner Societies throughout Germany,

One of Joseph Hoffmann's models for Bayreuth, 1876—the first act of Die Walküre.

Upon seeing the texts for the Ring Cycle, King Ludwig II of Bavaria became Wagner's main benefactor—but would remain so only as long as the king held all rights to the Operas.

and Ludwig in the end came through with a sizable advance.

On August 13, 1876, *Das Rheingold* opened the first season at Bayreuth. Prominent in the cast, as one of the Rhinemaidens, was Lilli Lehmann, who would one day graduate to Brünnhilde, thus securing her place in opera history. The festival closed that summer with a substantial deficit. It would be six years before another opera surfaced at Bayreuth (*Parsifal*, in 1882), and the *Ring* itself would not reappear until 1896. The composer's plans for a Bayreuth music school would never come to fruition. Still, in the summer of 1876, Wagner had triumphed.

The 1882 *Parsifal* was received ecstatically, and the Bayreuth festival became at long last a financial success. Wagner never lived to see his other works presented there. On February 13, 1883, on vacation in Venice, while at his desk, working on an essay, he suffered a fatal heart attack. Cosima proved a formidable keeper of the flame, supervising every facet of the festival's productions until 1908, when the reins were taken by her son, Siegfried. In 1930 she died at age ninety-two.

Although she would take certain liberties with future

Rhinemaidens seemingly swam in mid air thanks to stagehands' magic, Bayreuth, 1876.

productions of the *Ring*, Cosima remained true to Wagner's doggedly representational staging concepts. This posed all manner of practical difficulties. In the original 1876 *Rheingold*, the Rhinemaidens were held aloft on tall poles fastened to a stage truck; the poles moved up and down, sliding the Rhinemaidens around like merry-go-round horses. Eventually, because the singers suffered from acrophobia as well as motion sickness, the task fell to members of the *corps de ballet*, with the singing done offstage. Not until the 1950s, when Wieland Wagner, the composer's grandson, took over the festival, was a less literal-minded approach adopted. The Valkyries no longer "rode"; Fricka made her Act II entrance in *Die Walküre* minus her ram-drawn chariot, and Brünnhilde no longer had to engage in a battle of wills with her horse, Grane. Light and shadow were used to create all manner of effects. The principal stage setting became an exaggeratedly raked platform, the "Bayreuth disk," representing the universal rather than the specific. In recent years, as opera has increasingly become a director's medium, the *Ring* is often presented as a political or social allegory. In 1989, Deutsche Oper Berlin staged it in an underground time tunnel, inspired by Washington, D.C.'s subway system, complete with Valkyries in leather biker jackets and chains—a sort of Nordic miniskirt mob. But traditional productions—such as the Metropolitan Opera's current one, telecast in the spring of 1990—still abound.

Valkyrie costumes for the 1876 Bayreuth production by Carl Emil Doepler.

What would Wagner have thought of DC Comics' *The Ring of the Nibelung*? Since the original Bayreuth staging was never worked out to his satisfaction, perhaps he would have found Gil Kane's and Roy Thomas's pages liberating. Crucial flashbacks—most memorably, the stranger thrusting his sword into the ash tree at Sieglinde's and Hunding's wedding—impossible to show onstage, are worked out by Kane and Thomas with marvelous flair and detail. And the dragon is shown in all its ferocious majesty (probably Wagner would be especially pleased by this, for back in 1876 the dragon was manufactured in London and shipped to Bayreuth in sections, but the neck never arrived, having mistakenly been sent to *Beirut*).

Who knows? With the *Ring* now on television and in the comics, perhaps the door is open for Wagner's epic

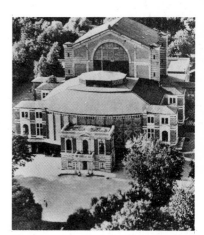

The theatre in Bayreuth, Bavaria—where it all began.

In 1902 Siegfried slays Fafner on a ramp as the dragon's vocal counterpart sings below the stage at the Paris Opéra.

cycle to reach a far wider audience than the composer could possibly have conceived of—via film. Perhaps we will yet see Steven Spielberg's vision of the *Ring*. Dream cast: Jason Robards as Wotan, Glenn Close as Fricka, Anjelica Huston as Brünnhilde, and as Siegfried—who else? Arnold Schwarzenegger. ❦

Photos on page 8, 9, 11, top of 12, and top of 15 courtesy of Motley Books Ltd.

Photos on page 10 and bottom of 12 courtesy of Raymond Mander and Joe Mitchenson Theater Collection.

Photos on page 13, 14, bottom of 15, and 16 courtesy of Opera News Magazine.

THE RHINEGOLD

IN THE DAY-SPRING OF THE AGES, THERE WAS NEITHER SEA NOR SHORE, HEAVEN NOR EARTH, BUT ONLY A VAST, YAWNING ABYSS...

...BOUNDED ON THE ONE SIDE BY HEAT AND FLAME...

...ON THE OTHER BY FREEZING MISTS.

AS FIRE MET ICE, ABOVE THE VOID, WARMED DROPS OF MOISTURE BEGAN TO FALL INTO THE GAPING CHASM.

OVER TIME, THE DROPS QUICKENED, HARDENED...

IN DAYS SOON AFTER WERE
MAN AND WOMAN MADE,
BY WOTAN AND HIS BROTHERS
HONER AND LODUR, FROM
SPLINTERS OF WOOD THEY
FOUND FLOATING UPON THE
WATER.

FROM THIS PAIR ARE DESCENDED
ALL THE HUMAN RACE, WHOSE
HABITATION IS CALLED MIDGARD.

THEN DID WOTAN AND HIS NEW RACE
OF GODS SET THEIR EYES UPON
THE HEIGHTS, WHERE THEY WOULD
RAISE A HALL OF THE VALIANT,
TO WHICH THE BRAVEST OF
HUMAN WARRIORS WOULD BE
TAKEN WHEN SLAIN IN BATTLE.

AND TO THE RIVER RHINE, WHICH
FLOWS GREEN AS EMERALDS
TOWARD THE SEA THAT CIRCLES
THE WORLD, WOTAN CONSIGNED
A HOARD OF GOLD WHOSE
MAGIC EVEN HE COULD NEVER
FULLY MASTER.

THUS ARE TIME'S BEGINNINGS
AND ITS END INEXTRICABLY
ENTWINED.

FOR, BELOW THE RIVER'S WAVES, UNDULATING WATERS DO SLOWLY RESOLVE THEMSELVES INTO A CLOUD OF MIST WHICH GROWS EVER FINER AS IT DESCENDS...

...TILL, NEAR THE BOTTOM OF THE RHINE, A SPACE THE HEIGHT OF A MAN STANDS FREE AND DRY.

ABOVE THAT DARKENING GLOOM, THREE GRACEFUL FIGURES FLIT LIKE GLISTENING GODDESSES THROUGH THE WATERS.

THE RHINE-MAIDENS.

ROCK YE OUR CRADLE!

HO, MY WILD SISTERS--

ROLL, YE BILLOWS!

BADLY YOU GUARD THE SLEEPING GOLD, WOGLINDE.

WELLGUNDE! WATCH WITH MORE ZEAL, OR YOU'LL PAY FOR YOUR SPORTING!

AND YOU, DEAR FLOSSHILDE, WERE EVER TOO SERIOUS!

HELLO, BRIGHT NYMPHS!

HOW INVITING YOU LOOK!

FROM NIBELHEIM'S NIGHT I'D GLADLY COME NEAR, IF YOU'D BE KIND TO ME!

HEI! SOMEONE CALLS TO US!

FROM BELOW-- AMID THE SHADOWS!

AHAHAHAHA

S-SPARE THE LIFE OF P-POOR LOGE, TERRIBLE DRAGON!

YOU ARE CONVINCED?

NOTHING SIMPLER, DULLARD! WATCH!

"CREEP AND CRAWL THERE--"

YES, BUT-- CAN YOU ALSO TURN INTO SOMETHING TINY, TO SLIP AWAY FROM YOUR FOES--

-- OR IS THAT, AS I SUSPECT, BEYOND EVEN YOUR POWERS?

"--CROOKED TOAD!"

YOU DID--

--VERY WELL!

GRONNK

I-- I AM CAUGHT!

MY CURSE-- UPON YOU BOTH!

NOW SWIFTLY UP...

...WHEN YOU BUT LOOSEN MY HANDS.

BY SECRET COMMAND, THE NIBELUNGS ARE CALLED TO HIS PLACE.

ALREADY I CAN HEAR THEM COMING.

...THERE! THE PRICE IS PAID--NOW LET ME DEPART!

AND MY HELMET-- GIVE THAT TO ME, ALSO!

NAY! THE PLUNDER MUST PAY FOR THE PARDON.

ACCURSED THIEF!

PATIENCE, NIBELUNG! HE WHO MOLDED THAT HELM CAN MOLD ME ANOTHER!

ALBERICH NOW OWNS NOTHING AT ALL.

UNBIND, YOU TYRANTS, HIS BONDS!

OUGHT I TO FREE HIM, WOTAN?

ARE YOU NOW CONTENT?

A GOLDEN RING CIRCLES YOUR FINGER, GNOME...

HO! LET THE PILE BE MORE *TIGHTLY* PACKED!

I CAN STILL *SEE* THE GODDESS THROUGH THE *CRANNIES.*

COME! THIS GAP MUST BE *CLOSED!*

DO YOU WANT TO *MEASURE,* FAFNER?

THEN MEASURE *YOUR* STRENGTH AGAINST *MINE--!*

CALM YOURSELF! I THINK SHE IS FINALLY HIDDEN.

NAY! HER *GOLDEN HAIR* STILL SHINES THROUGH!

BUT THE HOARD IS SPENT...

THAT THING *YONDER*--THROW IT ON THE PILE!

EVEN...

...THE *TARNHELM...?*

MAKE HASTE, OR ELSE--

LET IT GO, ALSO.

AT LAST WE HAVE FINISHED.

HAVE YOU NOW ENOUGH, GIANTS?

HOLD! HER EYES BEAM LIKE STARS UPON ME THROUGH THAT SINGLE CHINK!

WHILE I BEHOLD THOSE SWEET, SAD EYES, HOW CAN I EVER PART FROM HER?

AND ON *WOTAN'S FINGER* STILL GLEAMS A *GOLDEN RING!*

LET *THAT* CLOSE UP THE CREVICE!

TO ME, FREIA! YOU ARE...

...FREE.

MORE ON THE *MAID* THAN ON THE *GOLD* WERE YOUR EYES SET, BROTHER.

THUS IT IS ONLY FIT THAT MOST OF THE GOLD BE *MINE!*

LET HIM *HAVE* THE HOARD, FASOLT.

HOLD ON TO WHAT MATTERS -- THE RING!

HE'S RIGHT!

STAY BACK, FAFNER! MINE IS THE RING!

I LOST FOR IT FREIA'S SMILE!

NO!

THE RING IS MINE!

KRAKK

NOW, BROTHER--

--FEAST YOU ONLY UPON FREIA'S SMILE--

THUK

--FOR *NO MORE* SHALL YOU EVER TOUCH THE *RING!*

BOOK TWO

THE VALKYRIE

HUNDING?

HERE, WAYFARER...

WATER.

RELIEF FOR YOUR PARCHED LIPS.

ENOUGH. MY THIRST IS QUENCHED...

BUT *WHO* IS THIS LOVELY ONE WHO COMFORTS ME?

THIS HOUSE--

--AND THIS WIFE--

--BELONG TO *HUNDING*.

REST HERE, AS HIS GUEST, UNTIL HE COMES HOME.

I...WILL STAY.

YOUR HUSBAND WILL SURELY GRANT SHELTER TO A WOUNDED, WEAPON-LESS STRANGER.

YOU'RE WOUNDED?

QUICKLY--SHOW ME, AND I'LL--

THEY'RE ONLY SCRATCHES.

IF MY SWORD AND SHIELD HAD BEEN HALF AS STRONG AS MY ARM, I'D HAVE *VANQUISHED* MY ENEMY.

BUT BOTH WERE SPLINTERED-- SO I FLED, PURSUED BY STORM AND FOE ALIKE.

AT LAST, DARKNESS COVERED ME...

...YET NOW THE *SUN* LAUGHS ONCE MORE.

SHE GAVE ME WATER AND SHELTER.

WOULD YOU *CHIDE* HER FOR THAT?

WOMAN--

-- SET THE MEAL FOR US MEN!

YES, HUSBAND.

SACRED, STRANGER, IS MY HEARTH.

SACRED, TOO, IS MY HOME-- SO TREAT IT THUS.

... YOU MUST HAVE COME *FAR*, YET YOU HAVE NO HORSE. FROM WHERE DID YOU COME?

I CAME HERE BY A ROAD UNKNOWN... TO A PLACE I KNOW NO BETTER.

I'D BE HAPPY IF YOU CAN *TELL* ME WHERE I'VE WANDERED.

IT'S UNDER *HUNDING'S* ROOF YOU SIT.

AND IF YOU GO *WESTWARD* WHEN YOU DEPART--

-- YOU'LL FIND THE *KINSMEN* WHO GUARD HUNDING'S HONOR.

HOW LIKE TO MY *WIFE'S* HIS FEATURES ARE!

IN HIS EYES, AS IN HERS, GLEAMS THE GUILE OF THE SERPENT!

"ENEMIES ON ALL SIDES ROSE AND ASSAILED ME--

"--TILL SWORD AND SHIELD WERE HEWN, AT LAST, FROM MY HAND.

"'THEN, STANDING WEAPONLESS AND WOUNDED--

"-- I BEHELD THE MAID *DIE* BY THE HAND OF THE DEAD GROOM'S KIN.

"NO REASON TO GO ON FIGHTING, WHEN SHE LAY DEAD BESIDE THE HUSBAND SHE NEVER KNEW...

"SO I FLED ON FOOT FROM THE KILL-MADDENED HOST."

ARM YOURSELF WITH YOUR TRUSTIEST WEAPON--

--FOR YOU WILL SORELY *NEED* IT, COME THE SUNRISE!

YOU HAVE HEARD MY WORDS.

BE ON YOUR GUARD!

ONCE, MY FATHER TOLD ME-- WHEN MOST NEEDED, A *SWORD* I WOULD FIND AND WIELD.

THE *WOMAN* FOR WHOM I LONG-- SHE WHOSE CHARM BOTH WOUNDS AND DELIGHTS--IS HELD IN THRALL BY THE NEIDUNG WHO MOCKS A WEAPONLESS FOE.

FATHER, O' MY FATHER-- WHERE IS YOUR SWORD--

--THAT STOUT SWORD TO BE SWUNG IN BATTLE, WHEN RAGE BURSTS FORTH FROM MY BREAST?

EH? WHAT *BRIGHT GLEAM* IS THAT, REFLECTED FROM THE TRUNK OF THE ASH-TREE THAT SKEWERS THIS HOUSE?

IS IT THE *LOOK* THAT LINGERED BEHIND, WHEN *HUNDING'S WIFE* WENT FORTH FROM THE HALL?

ARE YOU ASLEEP, GUEST?

"HUNDING'S KINSMEN HAD ASSEMBLED IN THIS VERY PLACE, TO HONOR HIS WEDDING."

"AND *I*? SADLY I WATCHED, THROUGH ALL THEIR CAROUSING--"

"--WHEN, OF A SUDDEN, A *STRANGER* ENTERED."

"HE WAS AN OLD AND GREY-CLOAKED MAN-- SO SLOUCHED HIS HAT THAT ONE OF HIS EYES WAS HIDDEN.

"BUT THE OTHER EYE FLASHED SO THAT ALL DID *FEAR* IT!"

"I ALONE, WHEN I LOOKED AT HIM, FELT *SORROW* AND *SOLACE*, ALL IN ONE.

"GLANCING AT ME, HE SCOWLED AT ALL THE OTHERS--

"--AS HE SWUNG THE GREAT *SWORD* IN HIS HANDS--

"-- AND PLUNGED IT *UP TO THE HILT* INTO THE ASH-TREE'S STEM!"

-- THAT *VOLSUNG BLOOD* MAY FLOURISH FOREVER!

"THE *RING* HE MADE OF THE GOLD, I *STOLE* FROM HIM BY CUNNING -- BUT I RESTORED IT NOT TO THE RHINE.

"RATHER, IT PAID THE PRICE OF *VALHALLA*, THE CASTLE A PAIR OF GIANTS HAD BUILT FOR ME.

"*VALHALLA* -- FROM WHICH I COMMAND THE WORLD!

"*ERDA*, THE HOLY -- SHE WHO KNOWS ALL THAT EVER WAS -- WARNED ME CONCERNING THE RING -- PROPHESYING *DOOM EVERLASTING*.

"I WOULD HAVE LEARNED MORE, BUT SHE FADED FROM SIGHT.

"AT THIS, MY GLADNESS OF HEART WAS GONE.

"MY ONE DESIRE -- WAS TO *KNOW*.

"TO THE *EARTH'S WOMB* I WENT THEN...

"... AND, BY LOVE'S MAGIC POWER, I *VANQUISHED* ERDA, AND LEARNED HER SECRETS.

"YET, FOR THIS, THE WORLD'S WISEST WOMAN EXACTED A *FEE* OF ME."

SHE BORE ME *YOU*, BRUNNHILDE.

YOU -- AND YOUR *EIGHT VALKYRIE SISTERS*.

"WITH YOU SHIELD-MAIDENS, I HOPED TO AVERT THE *DOOM* WHICH ERDA HAD FORETOLD -- THE *TWILIGHT OF THE GODS.*

"THAT OUR FOES MIGHT FIND US STRONG, I HAD YOU VALKYRIE BRING ME THE MOST VALIANT OF *FALLEN WARRIORS.*

"AYE, YOUR DUTY WAS TO DRIVE MEN ON TO *SAVAGE WAR* -- AND THUS TO THEIR *DEATHS* -- "

-- SO THAT *HOSTS OF DAUNTLESS HEROES* MIGHT BE GATHERED IN VALHALLA, AGAINST THAT *FINAL BATTLE!*

AND *MANY A ONE* HAVE WE BROUGHT -- SO WHY DO YOU *FEAR?*

ERDA ALSO FORETOLD THAT, THROUGH VENGEFUL *ALBERICH,* OUR END MAY YET BEFALL US!

IF HE EVER REGAINS THE *RING,* HE COULD USE ITS RUNES TO MAKE MY VERY *HEROES* WAGE WAR UPON ME!

AND SO, ALARMED, I RE-SOLVED TO *WREST* THE RING FROM HE WHO *POSSESSES* IT!

"*FAFNER,* THE GIANT WHO SLEW HIS BROTHER FOR THE RHINEGOLD I PAID THEM, NOW GUARDS HIS HORDE IN THE FORM OF A FEARSOME *DRAGON.*

"THE *RING,* AT LEAST, I MUST RECOVER -- BUT I CANNOT STRIKE ONE PROTECTED BY *MY OWN OATH.*

"AH, BUT A *HERO* NEVER HELPED BY MY FAVOR -- ACTING SOLELY ON HIS *OWN* -- *HE* COULD ACHIEVE WHAT I MUST NOT!

"THINKING MYSELF SO VERY CLEVER, I ROAMED THE FOREST WITH YOUNG *SIEGMUND,* EVER GOADING HIM TO *REBEL* AGAINST THE GODS.

"NOW, HE HAS THE *SWORD* HE NEEDS -- BUT MY GODDESS WIFE KNOWS I *FORGED* IT FOR HIM, EVEN *LED* HIM TO IT.

"AND SO I NOW MUST BEND MY WILL TO *FRICKA'S* WISHES!"

SPEAK NOT TO ME OF THE VOLSUNG RACE!

RENOUNCING YOU, I HAVE RENOUNCED *THEM*, AS WELL!

IN *DEEP SLUMBER* YOU SHALL BE CAST--

--TO BECOME A MORTAL *WIFE* TO *ANY MAN* WHO FINDS AND WAKES YOU FROM THAT SLEEP!

IF CHAINS OF SLEEP MUST BIND ME, SIRE, I PLEAD BUT *ONE BOON*--

--SHIELD ME WITH *SOUL-DAUNTING TERRORS* --THAT BY A FEARLESS *HERO* ALONE, UPON THIS ROCK, I MAY BE REACHED.

CRUSH ME HERE-- PIERCE ME WITH YOUR SPEAR--

--BUT DO NOT EXPOSE ME TO SUCH MON- STROUS *SHAME!*

YOU ASK TOO MUCH!

LET THOSE EYES SO RADIANT AND FAIR TAKE THIS LAST KISS OF FOND FAREWELL.

ON HAPPIER *MORTAL* MAY THEY YET SHINE.

ON ME, THE HAPLESS IMMORTAL, THEY MUST CLOSE FOREVER.

THUS DO I KISS YOUR GODHOOD AWAY.

YET, IF I MUST LOSE YOU, WHOM I HAVE LOVED SO--

--FOR YOU SHALL BURN A *BRIDAL FIRE* BRIGHTER THAN ANY THAT EVER FLARED BEFORE--

--THAT COWARDS AND *FAINTHEARTS* EVER SHALL FLEE *BRUNNHILDE'S ROCK!*

BOOK THREE

SIEGFRIED

G-GET THAT BEAST OUT OF HERE, SIEGFRIED!

I WANT NO B-BEAR IN H-HERE!

I COME THUS PAIRED, OLD MIME-- THE BETTER TO PINCH YOU IF YOU'VE NOT DONE WHAT YOU SHOULD!

BRUIN-- ASK HIM NICELY FOR THE SWORD!

AROOOOOO

WELL? YOU HEARD HIM.

IF TH-THAT'S WHAT YOU WANT-- THEN LET HIM GO!

HERE LIES THE WEAPON YOU WANT.

I FINISHED IT ONLY TODAY!

WHY, THEN, YOU ARE SAFE--

--FOR TODAY.

ON YOUR WAY, BRUIN!

I NEED YOU NO MORE.

HAHAHA

AND IS MY ONLY REWARD FOR ALL MY SACRIFICE TO BE A BOY'S HOT-TEMPERED HATRED?

YOU'VE TAUGHT ME MANY THINGS, MIME.

BUT WHAT YOU MOST WANTED ME TO LEARN HAS PROVED A LESSON YOU COULDN'T TEACH:

HOW TO ENDURE THE VERY SIGHT OF YOU!

YET YOU ALWAYS RETURN HERE!

THAT OUGHT TO SHOW YOU THAT OLD MIME IS DEAR TO YOUR HEART.

WHAT THE OLD BIRD IS TO THE YOUNG, FEEDING IT IN ITS NEST, 'TIL THE FLEDGLING CAN FLY AWAY--

--THAT IS WHAT MIME IS TO YOU--

--WHAT HE MUST AND ALWAYS SHALL BE!

IF YOU'RE SO CLEVER, THEN TELL ME ONE THING MORE:

WHEN TWO BIRDS SANG TOGETHER IN THE SPRING, YOU SAID THEY WERE HUSBAND AND WIFE...

I SAW YOUNG WOLVES AND FOXES-- SUCKLED BY THEIR MOTHER, WHILE THEIR FATHER BROUGHT THEM FOOD.

BUT WHERE IS YOUR DEAR, LOVING WIFE, MIME--

--THAT I MAY CALL YOUR MOTHER?

YOU... MUST TRUST WHAT I TELL YOU.

I AM YOUR FATHER AND MOTHER, IN ONE!

LIAR! WHEN I SPY MY OWN FACE IN THE BROOK, IT'S NO MORE LIKE YOURS THAN A FISH IS LIKE A TOAD.

THAT'S WHY I MUST ALWAYS RETURN HERE -- UNTIL YOU TELL ME WHO MY FATHER AND MOTHER WERE!

WHAT "FATHER"? WHAT "MOTHER"?

MEANINGLESS QUESTIONS!

YOU NEVER TELL ME ANYTHING --UNLESS YOU ARE FORCED TO.

GET UP! HURRY, MIME! IF YOU HAVE ANY SKILL LEFT AT ALL, *SHOW* IT NOW!

I SWEAR THAT THE SWORD SHALL BE MINE--THIS VERY DAY!

AND WH-WHAT WILL YOU DO WHEN IT'S FINISHED?

LEAVE THIS FOREST FOREVER-- FOR NOTHING KEEPS ME HERE.

I SHALL FLY FAR AWAY, MIME, BEHOLDING YOU NO MORE!

STOP, BOY! SIEGFRIED--!

A NEW AND *CROWNING* WOE!

HOW DO I HOLD THE BOY HERE--LONG ENOUGH TO LEAD HIM, AT THE PROPER TIME, TO *FAFNER'S LAIR?*

AND HOW DO I WELD THESE SPLINTERS OF OBSTINATE STEEL?

IN NO FURNACE FIRE CAN THEY BE M-MELTED-- NOR CAN MY HAMMER COPE WITH THEIR H-HARDNESS!

ALL THE NIBELUNG'S HATE AND TOIL AND SWEAT CANNOT MAKE *"NEEDFUL"* N-NEW AGAIN--

--NOR FORGE THE S-SWORD-- INTO A WH-WHOLE--!

ALL HAIL, CUNNING SMITH!

A WAYWORN *GUEST* CRAVES A SEAT BY YOUR HEARTH.

"NEEDFUL"-- CONQUERING SWORD!

ONCE MORE TO LIFE I HAVE AWAKENED YOU!

SSSSSSS

WOE TO ALL ROBBERS-- ALL TRAITORS-- ALL ROGUES--!

LOOK YOU, MIME--

--THUS SUNDERS "NEEDFUL"--

SPLANNG

THE TARNHELM, IF HE BUT TAKE AND WEAR IT, WILL HELP HIM PERFORM DEEDS OF GREAT RENOWN--

--AND COULD HE BUT DISCOVER THE RING-- IT WOULD MAKE HIM LORD OF ALL THE WORLD!

MY THANKS, FEATHERED ONE, FOR THE ADVICE!

GLADLY WILL I ACT ON IT!

THIS, THEN, IS SURELY THE NIBELUNG HOARD OF WHICH THE BIRD SANG--

--THIS, THE *TARNHELM*--

-- AND THIS, THE *RING*--

--THAT WILL MAKE ME *RULER OF A WORLD!*

MIME, DEAR BROTHER--

--HAS LUST FOR *MY GOLD* PROVOKED YOUR GREED?

ACCURSED ALBERICH! WHAT I HAVE SLAVED AND TOILED TO WIN, YOU'LL NOT TAKE FROM ME!

OH? WAS IT YOU WHO ROBBED THE RHINE OF GOLD FOR THE RING, OR WROUGHT ITS MAGICAL *SPELL?*

NO--BUT WHO MADE THE *HELMET* WHICH CHANGES ITS WEARER'S FORM?

YOU COULD DO SO ONLY BECAUSE THE *RING* FORCED YOU TO MASTER YOUR CRAFT!

ERDA--FOUNTAIN OF KNOWLEDGE--OLD AS THE WORLD--

FROM HIDDEN DEPTHS, FROM CLOUD-COVERED CAVES, RISE AT MY CALL!

ALL-KNOWING ONE--AWAKE!

LOUD IS THE CALL--AND STRONG THE SPELL THAT DRAWS ME--

WHY HAVE YOU SUMMONED ERDA FORTH FROM DREAMS DARK AND WISE?

THE THREE NORNS ARE EVER WAKEFUL... TWINING THE ROPE AND DEFTLY WEAVING WHAT I DO KNOW.

'TIS THEY YOU SHOULD HAVE QUESTIONED, AND LET ME SLEEP.

THE NORNS WEAVE, AYE... BUT THEY CANNOT ALTER WHAT IS TO COME.

WHAT I WOULD BE TAUGHT IS HOW TO STAY FATE'S RUMBLING WHEEL.

WHY NOT SEEK COUNSEL FROM THE CHILD OF WOTAN AND ERDA--THE ONE I BORE YOU LONG AGO?

THE VALKYRIE, BRÜNNHILDE? SHE FLOUTED MY WILL, SEEKING TO SAVE A WARRIOR I WISHED SLAIN--

--SO I PRESSED FLAME-SHROUDED SLUMBER UPON HER EYES.

WILD, CONFUSED SEEMS THE WORLD, SINCE I HAVE AWAKENED.

LET ME DOWN TO THE DARK AGAIN!

NOT YET! IT WAS YOU WHO FORETOLD THE TWILIGHT DOOM OF THE GODS, AND THUS PUT FEAR INTO MY HEART.

NOW YOU MUST TELL ME HOW TO CONQUER THAT FEAR!

YOU'LL NOT ANSWER? THEN HEAR ME OUT!

THAT THE GODS MUST PERISH-- THAT THOUGHT NO LONGER DISMAYS ME.

INDEED, I NOW WILL OUR END!

ONCE, MAD WITH DISGUST, I GAVE OVER THE WORLD TO THE NIBELUNG'S HATE.

BUT NOW, TO THE VALIANT YOUNG VOLSUNG, I LEAVE IT WITH JOY!

A BOY BOLD AND FEARLESS--HELPED NOT BY WOTAN-- HAS WON THE NIBELUNG'S RING.

SINCE HE'LL BE BLESSED IN LOVE, THE CURSE PRONOUNCED BY LOVE RENOUNCING ALBERICH WILL FALL HARMLESS UPON HIM.

AND, AWAKEN BY THE HERO, OUR VALKYRIE CHILD SHALL ACHIEVE A DEED TO REDEEM THE WORLD!

WHATEVER THESE TWO MAY BRING TO PASS, I YIELD TO IT GLADLY!

DESCEND, THEN, ERDA, MOTHER OF FEAR AND THE WORLD'S SORROW--

DESCEND, AND LET YOUR WISDOM SLEEP FOREVER--

HAIL TO THEE, O SUN!

BRÜNNHILDE...

HAIL, SHIMMERING DAY! LONG HAVE I SLEPT!

WHAT HERO HAS BROKEN MY SLEEP?

I FORCED MY WAY THROUGH THE FIRES... AND WOKE YOU.

I AM SIEGFRIED.

SIEGFRIED-- HERO MOST BLESSED!

MY SHIELD SHELTERED YOUR LIFE BEFORE THAT LIFE WAS YOURS!

MY LOVE WAS YOURS-- EVEN BEFORE YOU WERE BORN!

YOUR WORDS ARE RAPTURE TO ME... THOUGH I CANNOT FATHOM THEIR MEANING.

I KNOW ONLY THAT, SINCE I REMOVED YOUR SHIELD AND HELMET, THE FLAMES ROARING AROUND THIS ROCK NOW BURN WITHIN MY BREAST, AS WELL.

O BEAUTIFUL MAIDEN --

--QUENCH THAT RAGING FIRE!

HOLD! NO GOD EVER EMBRACED ME SO-- AND *DYING WARRIORS* GREETED ME WITH AWE, WHEN I RODE FORTH FROM VALHALLA.

BUT NOW--*BITTER DISGRACE!*--YOU HAVE TAKEN MY HELMET--MY SHIELD--

--AND I AM *BRÜNNHILDE NO MORE!*

THEN, I'VE NOT YET TRULY BROKEN YOUR SLEEP.

AWAKE-- AND BE A *WOMAN* TO ME!

MY SENSES... THEY REEL!

WISDOM THAT WAS MINE-- WHY HAVE YOU FORSAKEN ME?

LET YOUR *NEW* WISDOM DRAW ITS LIGHT FROM YOUR LOVE FOR ME!

I BEG YOU--DO NOT CONQUER ME, LAUGHING HERO, AS YOU CONQUERED THE FIRE.

HAVE PITY ON ME--AND LEAVE ME *UNTOUCHED!*

I LOVE YOU.

WOULD ONLY THAT YOU LOVED ME!

BE MINE, BRÜNNHILDE!

OH, MY SIEGFRIED...

...I HAVE *ALWAYS* BEEN YOURS!

IF SO, THEN BE MINE *STILL*--AND MY NEWFOUND FEAR WILL VANISH!

MY BLOOD SURGES LIKE A TORRENT TOWARD YOU-- DON'T YOU FEEL IT?

DON'T YOU *FEAR* THIS WILD, LOVE-FRENZIED MAIDEN?

THE FEAR I NEVER LEARNED, BUT ONLY NOW, FROM YOU-- THAT FEAR, I'VE ALREADY *FORGOTTEN!*

BOOK FOUR

THE TWILIGHT OF THE GODS

ONE I KNOW OF-- NONE *NOBLER* IN ALL THE WORLD!

FAIR *BRÜNNHILDE* DWELLS ON SOARING ROCKS, ENCIRCLED BY FIRE.

HE WHO'D WIN HER MUST BREAK THROUGH THAT FLAME.

AND YOU THINK *MY* STRENGTH IS SUFFICIENT FOR THAT TASK?

ALAS, GUNTHER, THAT DEED IS RESERVED FOR THE VOLSUNG, *SIEGFRIED*--HE WHO SLEW A DRAGON TO WIN THE GOLD OF THE NIBELUNG.

WHAT? THEY SAY THAT TREASURE HOARD IS *PRICELESS!*

AYE! THE MAN WHO COULD *USE* ITS SPELL--WERE *LORD OF THE WORLD*, FOREVER-MORE!

SIEGMUND AND SIEGLINDA-- A TWIN-BORN PAIR WHOM FATE TURNED TO LOVERS-- WERE HIS STAR-CROSSED PARENTS...

...AND 'TIS HE THAT *YOU* SHOULD WED, DEAR GUTRINE!

I? YOU *MOCK* ME, HAGEN!

WHAT ARTS HAVE *I* TO WIN THE GREATEST HERO IN ALL THE WORLD?

REMEMBER THE *HERB-POTION* LOCKED AWAY IN YOUR JEWEL-CHEST, MY LADY?

IF SIEGFRIED DRANK OF IT, HE'D *FORGET* ANY WOMAN HE'D EVER SEEN BEFORE!

THEN, GUNTHER, WITH HIS HEART A PRISONER TO OUR SISTER, YOU'VE ONLY TO *ASK* HIM--

--AND HE WILL *GLADLY* GO WIN YOUR FIRE-HEMMED *BRIDE* FOR YOU!

WELL? WHAT DO YOU THINK OF MY PLAN?

MAY OUR MOTHER BE PRAISED, WHO GAVE US YOU FOR A HALF-BROTHER!

I MUST *SEE* THIS SIEGFRIED!

BUT HOW CAN HE BE FOUND, HAGEN?

MY *SWORD* AND *MYSELF* DO I OFFER, IN RETURN.

FOR MY OWN *BODY* IS ALL MY WEALTH I HAVE TO GIVE-- AND, AS I LIVE, IT GROWS EVER LESS.

OH? YET, RUMORS NAME YOU LORD OF THE *NIBELUNG DWARF'S TREASURE.*

THE HOARD? I ALMOST FORGOT ABOUT IT --

-- SO LIGHTLY DO I PRIZE ITS WORTH.

I LEFT IT LYING IN A CAVERN, WHERE A DRAGON ONCE STOOD WATCH.

AND YOU TOOK NOTHING AT ALL FROM SUCH A TREASURE?

ONLY...ONE THING...

...THIS *HELMET,* WHOSE VALUE I DO NOT EVEN KNOW.

WHY, 'TIS THE LEGENDARY *TARNHELM--*

-- THE CROWNING GEM OF THE NIBELUNG'S ART!

WORN ON YOUR HEAD, IT WILL *CHANGE YOUR SHAPE* TO WHATEVER YOU WILL!

IF YOU WISH TO BE *BORNE AFAR*--IN A FLASH, *LO!* YOU WILL BE THERE!

AND YOU TOOK... *NOTHING* ELSE?

WELL... THERE WAS A *RING.*

AND YOU'RE-- KEEPING IT *SAFE?*

A WOMAN MOST *WONDEROUS* IS.

NAY, SIEGFRIED, LET US NOT BARTER. ALL I HAVE IS BUT A POOR BAUBLE, MATCHED AGAINST YOUR TREASURE.

I WILL SERVE YOU GLADLY, WITH- OUT HOPE OF REWARD.

WELCOME, O GUEST, TO GIBICH'S HOUSE.

'TIS HIS *DAUGHTER* GIVES YOU TO DRINK.

IF ALL WERE *FORGOTTEN* THAT YOU TOLD ME, ONE LESSON I WOULD *NEVER* FORGET.

AND SO THIS FIRST *DRAUGHT*-- WITH *LOVE UNDYING*--

--*BRÜNNHILDE,* I DRINK TO THEE!

THEN LET THE *BLOOD-OATH* NOW BE SWORN!

"*QUICKENING BLOOD OF BLOSSOMING LIFE--*

"--*BRAVELY MIXED IN BROTHERLY LOVE--*

"--*IF BROKEN THIS BOND, OR FAITH-LESS THE FRIEND--LET HE WHO BREAKS IT PAY THE WAGE OF TREACHERY!*"

SEALED BE OUR BOND!

PLEDGED BE OUR FAITH!

HAGEN, WHY DID *YOU* NOT JOIN IN THE OATH?

SO I HOLD ALOOF FROM HOT-BLOODED BONDS.

MY BLOOD IS NOT SO PURE OR NOBLE AS YOURS.

LET THAT UNHAPPY CHURL BE, SIEGFRIED.

WILL YOU REST A WHILE, BEFORE WE BEGIN OUR QUEST?

NO. I AM EAGER THAT WE SHOULD DEPART--

--THE SOONER THAT I MAY RETURN TO GUTRUNE.

--I, WHOM LOVE HAS TRULY BLESSED WITH VIRTUOUS GUTRUNE!

WHAT WIZARD'S SPELL HAS WORKED THIS WOE?

I GAVE SIEGFRIED ALL MY RUNE-WISDOM, AND NOW I AM MERELY HIS BOOTY-- TO BE LIGHTLY GIVEN TO ANOTHER!

WILL NO ONE LEND A SWORD WITH WHICH I MAY SEVER MY UN-SEEN BONDS?

LEAVE THAT TO HAGEN, WRONGED ONE.

I WILL AVENGE YOU ON SIEGFRIED!

YOU?

A SINGLE FLASH OF HIS EYE AND ITS LIGHTNING-- AND YOUR COURAGE WOULD DESERT YOU!

BUT HIS OATH-LIES... THEY MAKE HIM VULNERABLE TO MY SPEAR!

TRUTH -- FALSEHOOD-- WHAT MATTER MERE WORDS?

SEEK FOR SOMETHING STRONGER, IF YOU WOULD WITHSTAND SUCH POWER AS HIS!

I KNOW WELL OF SIEGFRIED'S PROWESS IN BATTLE.

THEN WHISPER TO ME SOME SECRET WAY TO SPEED HIM TO HIS DOOM!

I TAUGHT HIM ALL THE RUNIC ARTS I KNOW TO PRESERVE HIS BODY FROM HARM.

WITHOUT HIS KNOWING IT, HE BEARS A CHARMED LIFE, AND WALKS ALL WRAPPED ABOUT WITH PROTECTING SPELLS.

THEN-- NO WEAPON FORGED COULD HARM HIM?

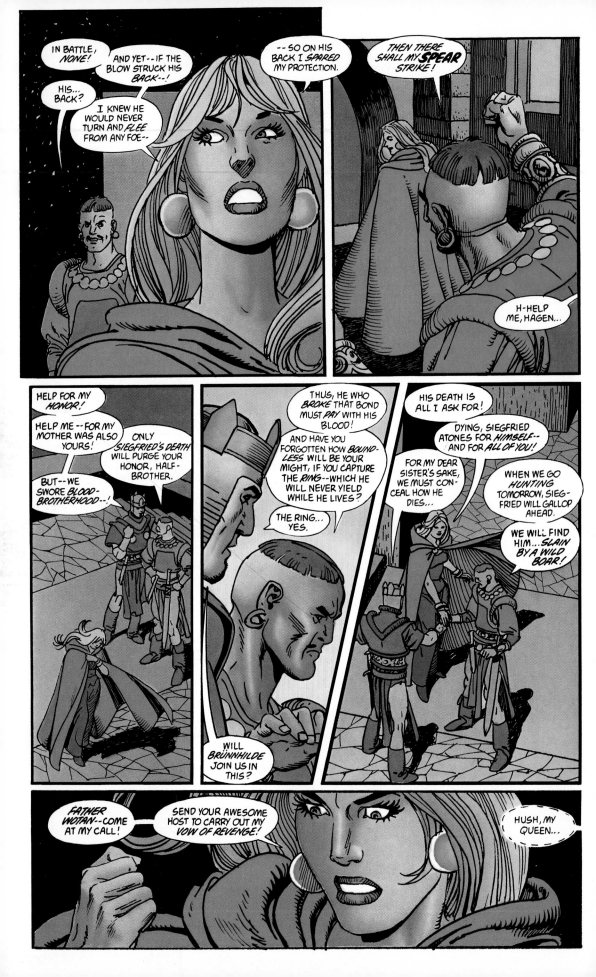

... THE *BRIDAL PROCESSION* COMES...

THE *DIE* IS CAST! SIEGFRIED'S FATE IS SEALED.

MINE WILL BE BOTH *RING* AND *HOARD OF GOLD* -- AND MINE SHALL I *HOLD* IT!

FATHER-- *ALBERICH*-- HEAR YOUR *SON!*

BID THE *NIBELUNG* HOST OBEY YOU ONCE AGAIN --

--THE *RING'S DREAD LORD!*

THOUGH THE *SUN* SENDS OUT ITS RAYS OF GLORY...

...HERE IN THE *RHINE* THERE IS ONLY *DARKNESS*...!

O SUN -- SEND US THE *HERO* WHO SHALL GIVE BACK TO US OUR STOLEN *GOLD!*

RHINEGOLD -- HOW BRIGHT ONCE WAS YOUR RADIANCE --

-- GLORIOUS STAR OF THE WATERS!

HOLD, SISTERS!

HE COMES!

SIEGFRIED!

HO, DOWN THERE, FROLICKSOME MAIDS!

HAVE YOU SEEN THE SHAGGY-HIDED *BEAST* I WAS PURSUING?

WHAT WILL YOU GIVE US IF WE TELL YOU?

I HAVE CAUGHT NOTHING YET, SO ASK WHAT YOU WILL.

AH! THAT TASTED GOOD!

YOU ARE QUIET TODAY, GUNTHER.

HERE -- DRINK! YOUR BLOOD-BROTHER OFFERS YOU THE HORN.

A...PALE WINE YOU HAVE POURED... BROTHER...

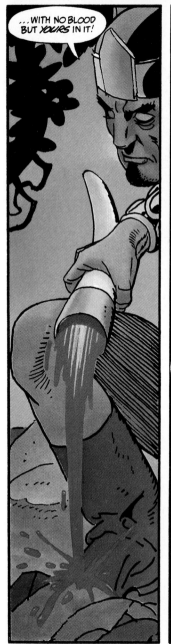

...WITH NO BLOOD BUT YOURS IN IT!

POOR, SAD GUNTHER.

PERHAPS A TALE OF MY BOYHOOD WILL CHEER UP WHAT BRÜNNHILDE HAS MARRED.

OUT OF GREED, A SURLY OLD DWARF NAMED MIME REARED ME, SO I COULD SLAY A DRAGON FOR HIM WHEN I GREW UP.

HE TAUGHT ME TO FORGE, AND FROM THE SPLINTERS OF MY FATHER'S BLADE I FASHIONED MY OWN SWORD, "NEEDFUL."

IN THE FOREST, I SLEW THE DRAGON FAFNER, WHO GUARDED THE NIBELUNG GOLD.

BUT WHEN I TOUCHED ITS BLOOD TO MY LIPS, I HEARD A BIRD SPEAKING OF THE TARNHELM --

-- AND OF THE RING WHICH COULD MAKE ME LORD OF THE WORLD.

WHEN I HAD OBTAINED BOTH, THAT SAME BIRD WARNED ME THAT MIME WAS NOW BENT ON MURDERING ME, FOR THE SAKE OF THE GOLD.

THE DWARF TRIED TO POISON ME WITH A DEADLY BREW --

...BUT HIS WORDS BETRAYED HIS DEEDS, AND MY SWORD STRETCHED HIM OUT DEAD.

HAH! THE STEEL HE HAD NOT FORGED, OLD MIME SOON *TASTED*, EH?

HERE! A DRINK FROM MY HORN -- TO REMIND YOU OF THINGS LONG FORGOTTEN.

DID THE BIRD TELL YOU ANYTHING ELSE?

AYE! IT SANG OF A *MOST GLORIOUS BRIDE* FOR ME--

-- ONE WHO SLEPT AMID SKY-JUTTING ROCKS, HER CHAMBER RINGED BY *FIRE!*

I SOON PASSED THROUGH THOSE FLAMES--

--AND THERE I FOUND, SLEEPING, A *WOMAN* BOTH ARMORED AND BEAUTIFUL!

I WOKE HER WITH MY KISS -- AND THEN--

--THEN, THE BURNING, SWEET EMBRACE OF *BRÜNNHILDE'S* RAPTUROUS ARMS!

WHAT ARE YOU SAYING?

KAWWWWW

KAWWW

KAWWW

DID YOU UNDERSTAND WHAT THOSE *RAVENS* SAID, SIEGFRIED?

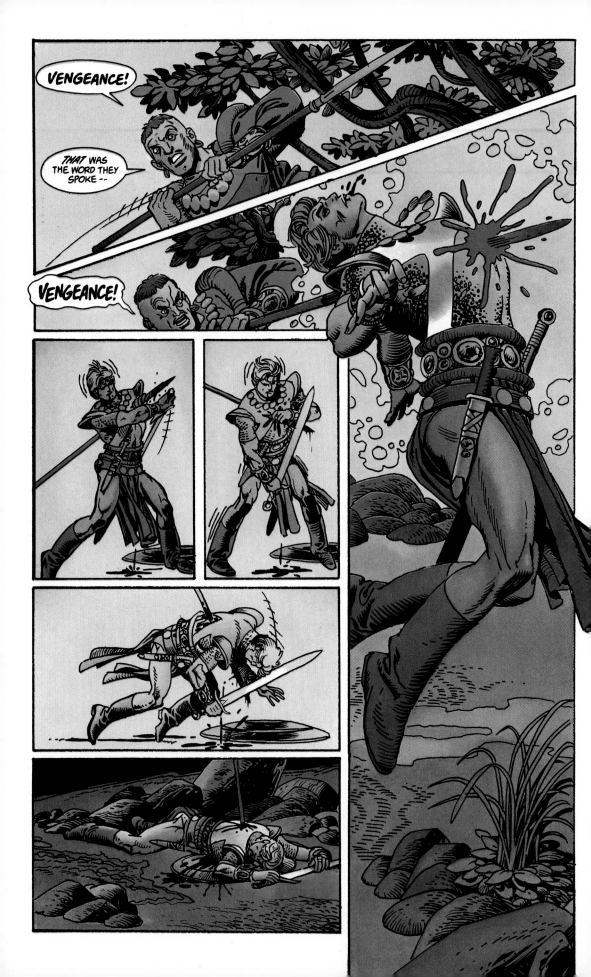

HAGEN-- WHAT HAVE YOU DONE?

I HAVE BUT BROUGHT *DEATH*, DEAR GUNTHER--

--TO A *BREAKER OF OATHS!*

BRÜNNHILDE...

MY...

...BRIDE...

WAS THAT *BRÜNNHILDE* I SAW GO DOWN-WARD TO THE RHINE?

OH, WHEN WILL *SIEGFRIED* RETURN?

HAGEN? WHAT IS WRONG?

I SAW THE *TORCHES*, BUT-- WHAT ARE THEY CARRYING?

A *WILD BOAR'S PREY* THEY BRING TO YOU, GENTLE SISTER--

--YOUR HUSBAND *SIEGFRIED*--

--SLAIN!

SIEGFRIED...?

YOU! FALSE-HEARTED BROTHER-- MURDERER OF MY HUSBAND!

NO! HAGEN IS THE ACCURSED "WILD BOAR" WHO DEALT THE HERO'S DEATH!

AND YOU REVILE ME FOR IT, NOW?

THEY HAVE SLAIN SIEGFRIED?

THEN--YES! I SLEW HIM WITH THE SPEAR BY WHICH HE FALSELY SWORE.

AND FOR MY PRIZE, I CLAIM-- THE RING!

AWAY! YOU'LL NOT HAVE WHAT RIGHTLY FALLS TO ME, NIBELUNG-SON!

I WILL SHOW YOU HOW THE SON OF THE NIBELUNG DEMANDS HIS OWN!

THE RING IS MINE!

MINE!

SILENCE YOUR CLAMORING!

NOW, FOR HER VENGEANCE, SIEGFRIED'S TRUE WIFE COMES--

--THE WOMAN ALL HAVE BETRAYED!